For Solomon, of course!

THIS IS A BORZOI BOOK PUBLISHED BY ALFRED A. KNOPF

Visit us on the Web! randomhousekids.com
Educators and librarians, for a variety of teaching tools,
visit us at RHTeachersLibrarians.com

Library of Congress Cataloging-in-Publication Data
Names: Valentine, Madeline, author.
Title: I want that nut! / Madeline Valentine.
Description: First Edition. | New York : Alfred A. Knopf, [2017] | Summary: "Mouse and Chipmunk covet the same nut."
—Provided by publisher
Identifiers: LCCN 2016019486 (print) | LCCN 2016059225 (ebook) | ISBN 978-1-101-94037-2 (trade) |
ISBN 978-1-101-94038-9 (lib. bdg.) | ISBN 978-1-101-94039-6 (ebook)
Subjects: | CYAC: Mice—Fiction. | Chipmunks—Fiction. | Greed—Fiction.
Classification: LCC PZ7.V25214 Iam 2017 (print) | LCC PZ7.V25214 (ebook) |
DDC [E]—dc23

The illustrations in this book were created using watercolor and pencil digitally arranged and tweaked.

MANUFACTURED IN CHINA
October 2017   10 9 8 7 6 5 4 3 2 1   First Edition

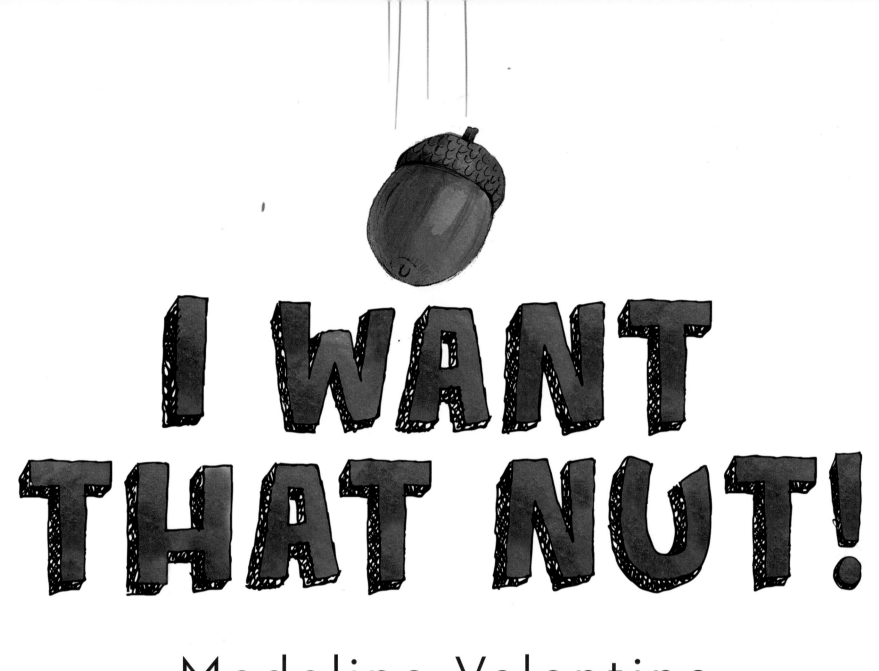

I WANT THAT NUT!

Madeline Valentine

Alfred A. Knopf · New York

Mouse and Chipmunk were playing together when they heard a *ker-plunk!*

They peeked through the bushes and saw . . .

a Nut!

A big,
beautiful
Nut.

Mouse looked
at the Nut.

Chipmunk looked
at the Nut.

Mouse and Chipmunk looked at each other.

Chipmunk took the Nut.

Chipmunk and the Nut were inseparable.

They played together.
They read together.
They lay in the grass
and stared at the
clouds together.

I want that Nut.

Mouse went to Chipmunk's house for a friendly visit. He very politely knocked on the door.

Mouse took the Nut.

Mouse and the Nut did everything together.
They played tic-tac-toe together.
They napped together.

They were having a dance party together . . .

when there was a knock on the door.

The visitor looked a *little* familiar.

Hello. I am the judge of the Most Beautiful Nut Contest. You may have heard of us. Do you have a Nut?
Yes!
Give me that Nut!

Mouse paused.

He looked *very closely*
at the visitor.

He handed the visitor the Nut.

Chipmunk and the Nut were having the *best* time together . . .

when Mouse stomped over.

Hand over that Nut!

THE NUT

IS MINE!

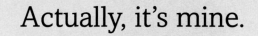

Actually, it's mine.

It fell out of my tree this morning. I've been looking for it all day.

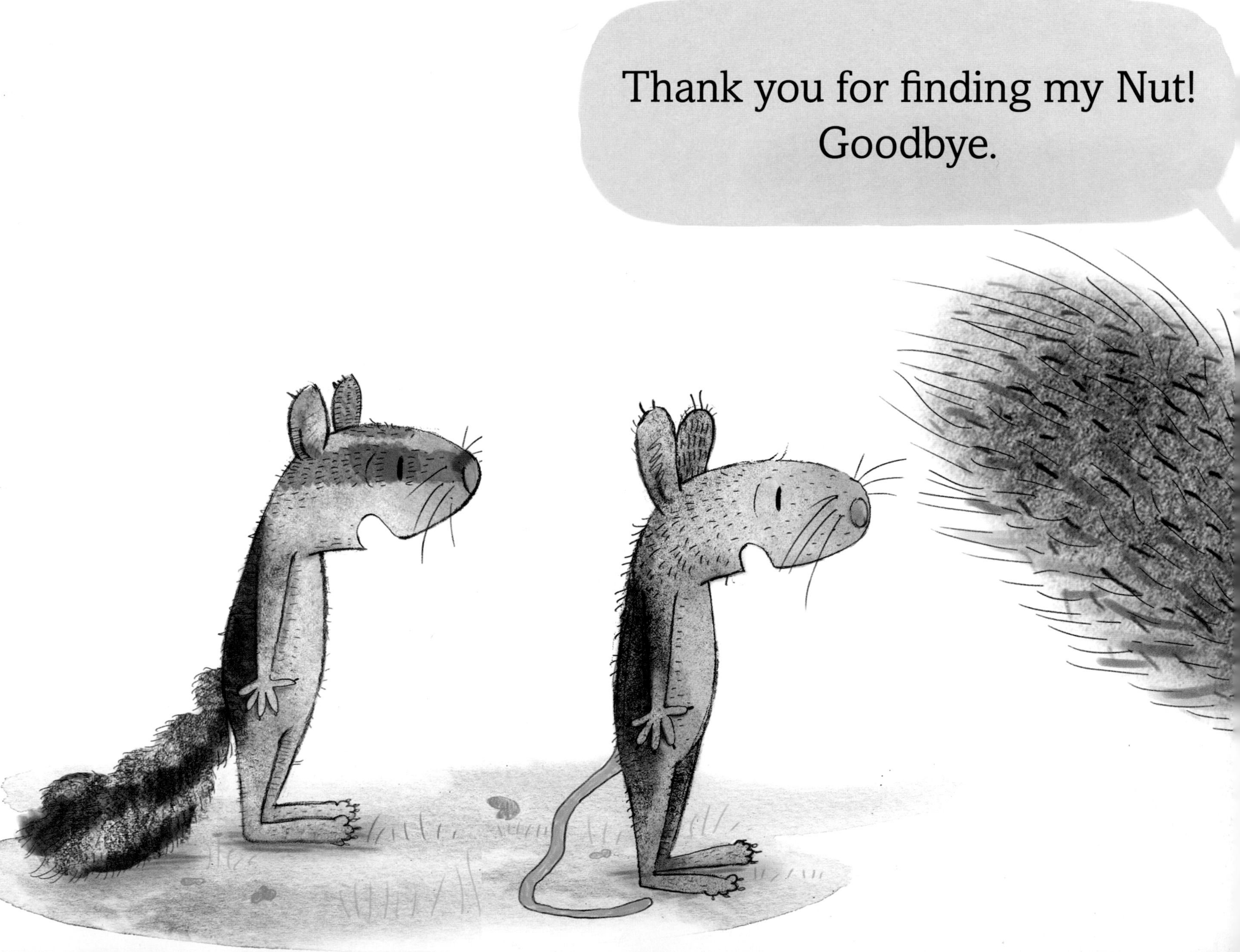
Thank you for finding my Nut!
Goodbye.

Mouse and Chipmunk sat down together.

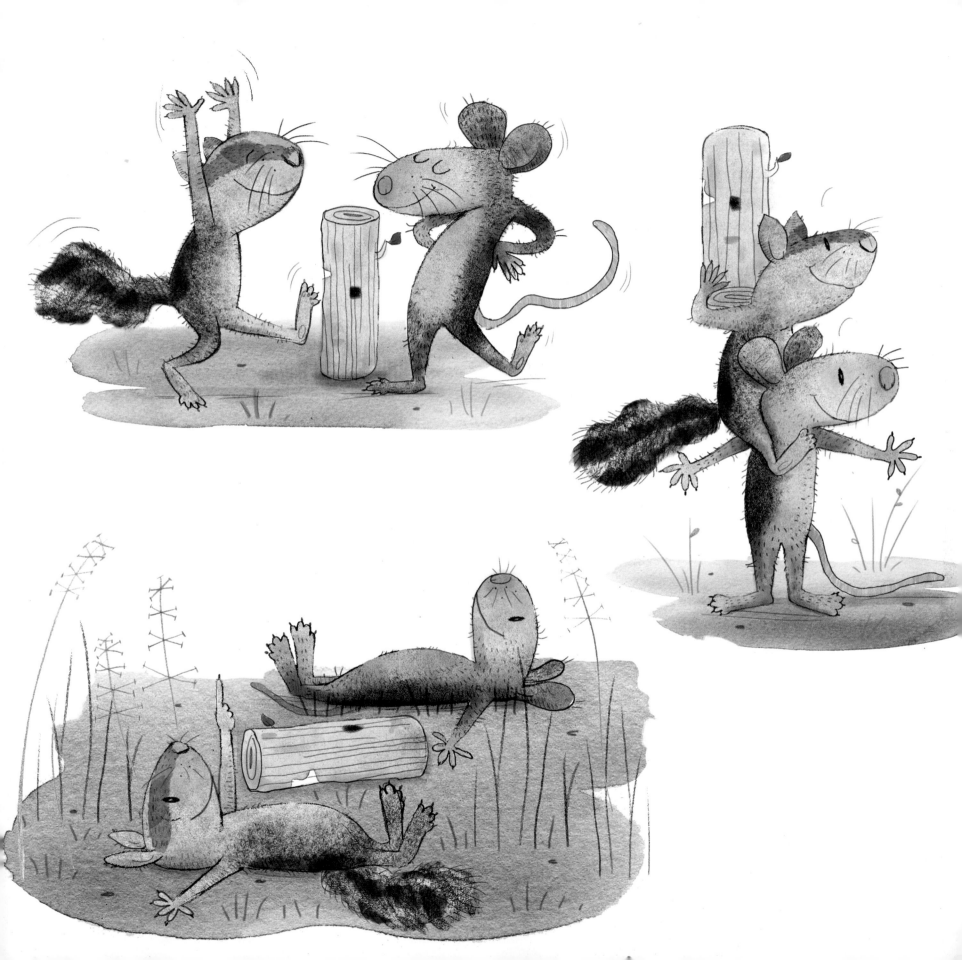

Mouse smiled at Chipmunk.
Chipmunk smiled at Mouse.

Mouse, Chipmunk, and the Log
had the *best* time together.